For Colden

First published in 2023 by Child's Play (International) Ltd
Ashworth Road, Bridgemead, Swindon SN5 7YD, UK

Published in USA in 2023 by Child's Play Inc
250 Minot Avenue, Auburn, Maine 04210

Distributed in Australia by Child's Play Australia Pty Ltd
Unit 10/20 Narabang Way, Belrose, Sydney, NSW 2085

ISBN 978-1-78628-623-9
SJ260722CPL09226239

Printed in Shenzhen, China

1 3 5 7 9 10 8 6 4 2

A catalogue record of this book
is available from the British Library

www.childs-play.com

CAT'S SEASONS

Airlie Anderson

It is summer. Cat and her kittens
are doing summery things.

They take in the warm sun.

Soon, summer is changing...

...to autumn.

Cat and her kittens play in the leaves.

Next, autumn turns...

...to winter.

Brrr, it's cold!

But playing in the snow is fun.

Winter finally gives way...

...to spring!

Everything is growing.

Spring turns to summer once again.

Uh-oh, a summer storm is coming!

Better hide!

BOOM!

Is it safe yet?

Yes, it is!

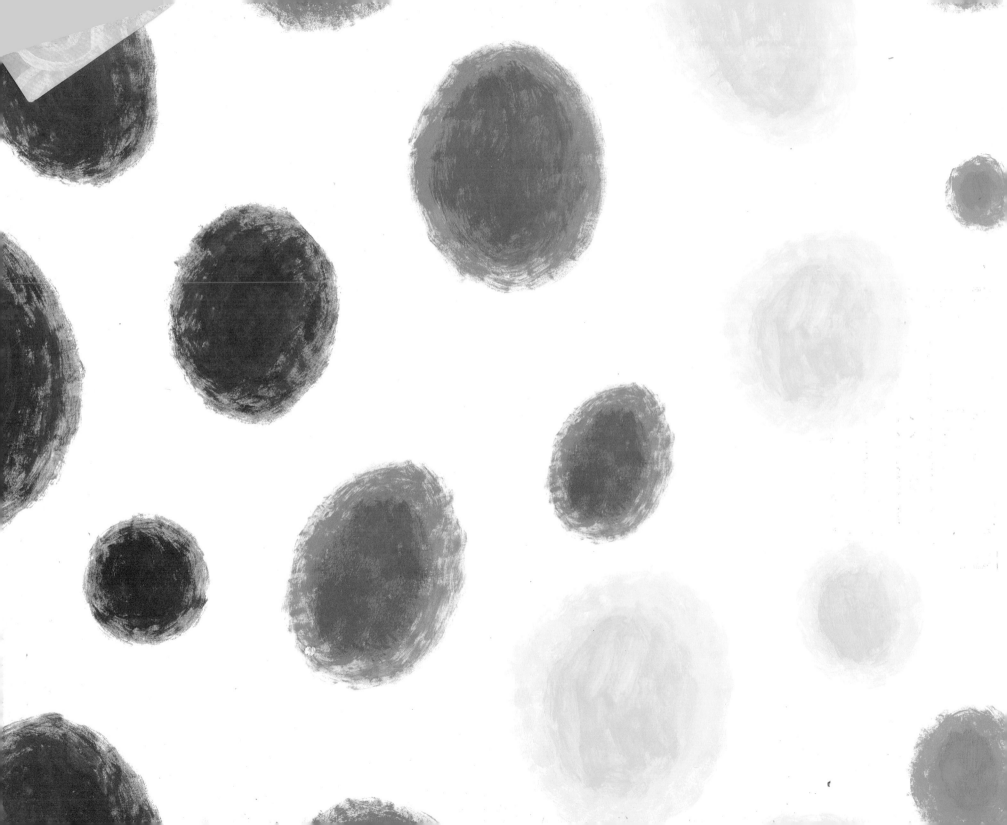